The Dream Eater

The Dream Eater

STORY BY CHRISTIAN GARRISON

PICTURES BY DIANE GOODE

Aladdin Books
Macmillan Publishing Company
New York

Collier Macmillan Publishers
London

Aladdin Books
Macmillan Publishing Company
866 Third Avenue, New York, NY 10022
Collier Macmillan Canada, Inc.

First Aladdin Edition 1986

Printed in USA

10 9 8

Library of Congress Cataloging-in-Publication Data
Garrison, Christian.
  The dream eater.
  Summary: Yukio spares the other villagers from recurring nightmares when he rescues a baku.
  [1. Dreams — Fiction.   2. Monsters — Fiction]
I. Goode, Diane, ill.   II. Title.
PZ7.G1848Dr   1986   [E]   85-26771
ISBN: 0-689-71058-5 (pbk.)

For Will
–C.G.

For my Uncle Guido
–D.G.

Yukio dreamed that he was being chased by a three-headed demon upon a dragon with twenty eyes. Just as the demon was about to devour him, Yukio woke from his sleep.

Over and over Yukio had the same dream. So he decided to sleep no more.

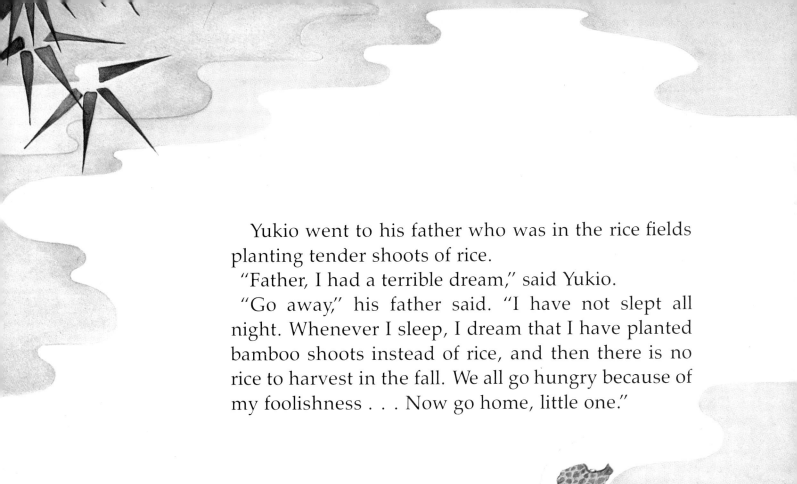

Yukio went to his father who was in the rice fields planting tender shoots of rice.

"Father, I had a terrible dream," said Yukio.

"Go away," his father said. "I have not slept all night. Whenever I sleep, I dream that I have planted bamboo shoots instead of rice, and then there is no rice to harvest in the fall. We all go hungry because of my foolishness . . . Now go home, little one."

Yukio went to his mother who was preparing rice balls for supper.

"Mother, I had a terrible dream," said Yukio.

"Everyone in the village has bad dreams," his mother said. "I have not slept for three nights. If I fall asleep, I dream that the winter snow has come and turned everything to ice. We are all so cold and cannot keep warm . . . Here. Take this rice ball and leave me alone."

Yukio went to his grandfather who was mending his fishing net.

"Grandfather, I had a terrible dream," said Yukio.

"Go away," said his grandfather. "It is just a time for bad dreams."

"Do you have bad dreams too?" Yukio asked.

"Yes," replied his grandfather. "I have them too. I dream that I am a golden fish swimming in a silver sea, and all at once I am caught up in a fisherman's net. No matter how I turn and twist I cannot get free."

"Oh, that certainly is a terrible dream to have," said Yukio.

"Go," his grandfather said. "Be by yourself."

"I will go to the river," Yukio thought. "It will not tell me to go away."

Yukio came upon Danjuro, the old samurai who guarded the river bridge. Danjuro was napping, but his sleep was an uneasy one. Suddenly he cried out, "Bandits! To arms! To arms!"

"Master samurai!" said Yukio. "It is only I, Yukio."

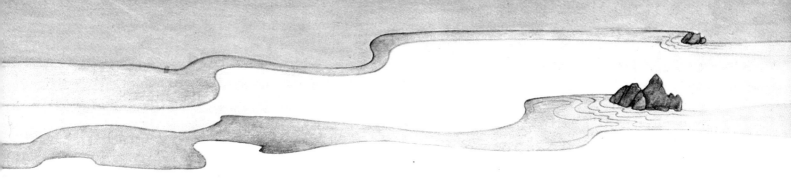

"Oh, " Danjuro sighed. "I was dreaming again . . . I dream that the village is being attacked by fierce bandits riding brimstone horses and shooting arrows of fire. I have only a sword of bamboo with which to fight. A bamboo sword is a foolish weapon for a samurai."

"Master Danjuro, I had a terrible dream too," said Yukio.

"Go away," said Danjuro sleepily.

Yukio went on his way to find a place by the river to sit and be alone.

On the river bank Yukio sat upon some stones and listened to the breezes rattle and tap the bamboo together. The water made sighing sounds on its way to the sea. Yukio longed to ride the river and sail away on oceans of sleep.

All at once, Yukio's eyes flew open. There at the water's edge he saw something he had never seen before. The strangest of creatures was drinking from the river when suddenly his front feet slipped on a wet stone.

KWOOSH!

The creature fell headfirst into the river. The cold rushing water pulled him under.

"Help! Help!" the creature cried.

Quickly Yukio searched for a way to save him.

"Help!" the creature cried out again.

Yukio found a strong vine which he threw out over the water. The creature took hold, and Yukio pulled him safely to the river bank.

"I owe you my life," the creature said.

"What are you?" Yukio asked.

"I am a baku and so hungry I think I shall die."

"I would be honored if you ate this rice ball," said Yukio.

"A baku does not eat such things."

"Oh," Yukio said. "What does a baku eat?"

"Dreams," said the baku. "Nightmares. I eat them. To a baku bad dreams are delicious."

Yukio clapped his hands in delight. "Come with me," he said, "and you shall be the fattest baku in all Japan!"

On their way to the village Yukio and the baku crossed the river bridge.

Danjuro's dream of bandits was visiting him again . . . but before his visions of battle could disturb Danjuro the baku gobbled up the bandits, brimstone horses, arrows of fire and all.

Old Danjuro settled down into a sleep so pleasant he smiled.

He started dreaming of springtime and of writing poems on bits of paper which he floated down the river like little boats with words on them.

In the village Yukio led the baku to his grandfather who had fallen asleep at his work. The grandfather dreamed of being caught in the fisherman's net once more. In one bite the baku ate all of his terrible nightmare.

Yukio's grandfather slept soundly for the first time in days.

He began to dream of Mount Fuji shining in the sun.

Soon Yukio's mother was no longer troubled by her dream of winter, for the baku ate his fill of that one. Yukio's mother dreamed about the warmth of summer and of gathering sweet cherries from the trees.

In his sleep Yukio's father no longer dreamed of planting bamboo shoots instead of rice, for the baku devoured that nightmare too. Yukio's father dreamed of tender rice plants blowing in the wind and of a plentiful harvest.

"Do not forget me, baku," said Yukio who could no longer hold his eyes open. When his dreams of demons and dragons came to him, the baku munched away on every morsel. He found Yukio's nightmare especially tasty.

Yukio dreamed of yellow butterflies fanning him on a hot summer's day.

By nightfall the villagers slept peacefully. And the baku, filled with all their bad dreams, was contented.